Troubletops
and the New Baby

First published in 2011 by Scholastic Children's Books
Euston House, 24 Eversholt Street
London NW1 1DB
a division of Scholastic Ltd
www.scholastic.co.uk

London ~ New York ~ Toronto ~ Sydney ~ Auckland
Mexico City ~ New Delhi ~ Hong Kong

Written by Katherine Halligan
Text copyright © 2011 Scholastic Children's Books
Illustrations copyright © 2011 Sean Julian

HB ISBN: 978 1407 115 44 3
PB ISBN: 978 1407 115 62 7

For Tom – KH
For Mum and Dad,
thanks for keeping me
out of trouble! – SJ

Troubletops
and the New Baby

BEWARE OF THE
MORGANUCODON

Katherine Halligan & Sean Julian

■SCHOLASTIC

Troubletops was **always** causing trouble.

He liked to paint pictures.

He liked to cook.

And he especially loved
to go exploring with Morgan.

Everywhere Troubletops went . . .

. . . trouble followed him.

"Here comes trouble!"
said his daddy.

"Here comes trouble!"
said his mummy.

But then came **real** trouble.
"We're going to have a baby,"
said his mummy.

And they did.

Everyone was too busy with Tinytops to notice
when trouble was coming.

They took Tinytops for walks. They changed her nappies.

They sang songs and gave her cuddles
and rocked her to sleep.

Troubletops felt left out.
He felt lonely.
He felt sad.

"What's the trouble, Troubletops?" asked Morgan.
"I'm not in trouble anymore!" said Troubletops.
"Everyone wants to play with Tinytops and no one notices me."

A big tear rolled down
his face and dripped
off the tip of his horn.

"I think I'll run away," sniffed Troubletops.
"Then they'll be sorry." So Troubletops packed a sack.
Morgan helped.

And when his mummy and daddy
were busy with Tinytops (again),
out Troubletops crept.

He went down the path,

BEWARE OF THE MORGANUCODON

over the log

through
the gate,

along the pavement,

and into the forest.

"There!" he thought. He waited by the tallest tree. There wasn't much trouble to get into, so he just sat quietly and thought.

Back at the cave, the Tops family
was all in a bother.
"Where is he?!" wailed his mummy.
"Our little boy!" wailed his daddy.
"Waaa!" wailed Tinytops.

"Excuse me!"
barked Morgan.

Out the Tops family ran. Down the path

along the pavement,

over the log,

through
the gate,

into the forest . . .

And there, under the tallest tree, was Troubletops.

"Troubletops!" cried his mummy.
"Our little boy!" cried his daddy.
"Yay!" shouted Tinytops.
Morgan just smiled.

And from that day on, his mummy and daddy always noticed when trouble was on its way.

"Here comes trouble!" smiled his mummy.

"There goes trouble!"
laughed his daddy.

But sometimes Troubletops didn't have time to get into **quite** as much trouble.

He was too busy with other things . . .

. . . Like keeping **Tinytops** out of trouble!

The End

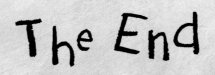